ICE FORCE

by Holly Kowitt
Illustrated by Jesus Redondo (pencil & ink)
and Mark Mones (colorist)

Special thanks to David Manis

ISBN 0-439-45186-8

Published by Scholastic Inc.

12 11 10 9 8 7 6 5 4 3 2 1 3 4 5 6 7 8/0

Printed in the U.S.A.
First printing, January 2003

SCHOLASTIC INC.

New York Toronto London Auck.
Mexico City New Delhi Hong Kong Buenos Aires

In Alaska, Duke, Gung-Ho, and Frostbite patrolled the icy mountains by helicopter.

When they finished their guard duty, they zoomed back to base camp.

At the base, a report came over the radio.

"This is Weather Station Alpha!" a scared voice said. "Our town has flooded! Please send help!"

Minutes later, the G.I. JOE team arrived.

"Help!" people cried.

Soon everybody was rescued — no problem for A Real American Hero!

One of the rescued men was a scientist. "There is strange weather at Desolation Peak," he warned.

The G.I. JOE team promised to check it out.

They parachuted into the mountains near Desolation Peak.

“Something is wrong here!” said Frostbite. “All the animals are leaving.”

The G.I. JOE team climbed Desolation Peak. Near the top, they saw a tall tower on a cliff.

"Look!" said Gung-Ho.

A powerful laser zapped the ice around the tower, melting huge chunks of it instantly!

Through his binoculars, Frostbite saw their enemies in the command tower. "That's COBRA Commander and Destro!" he said.

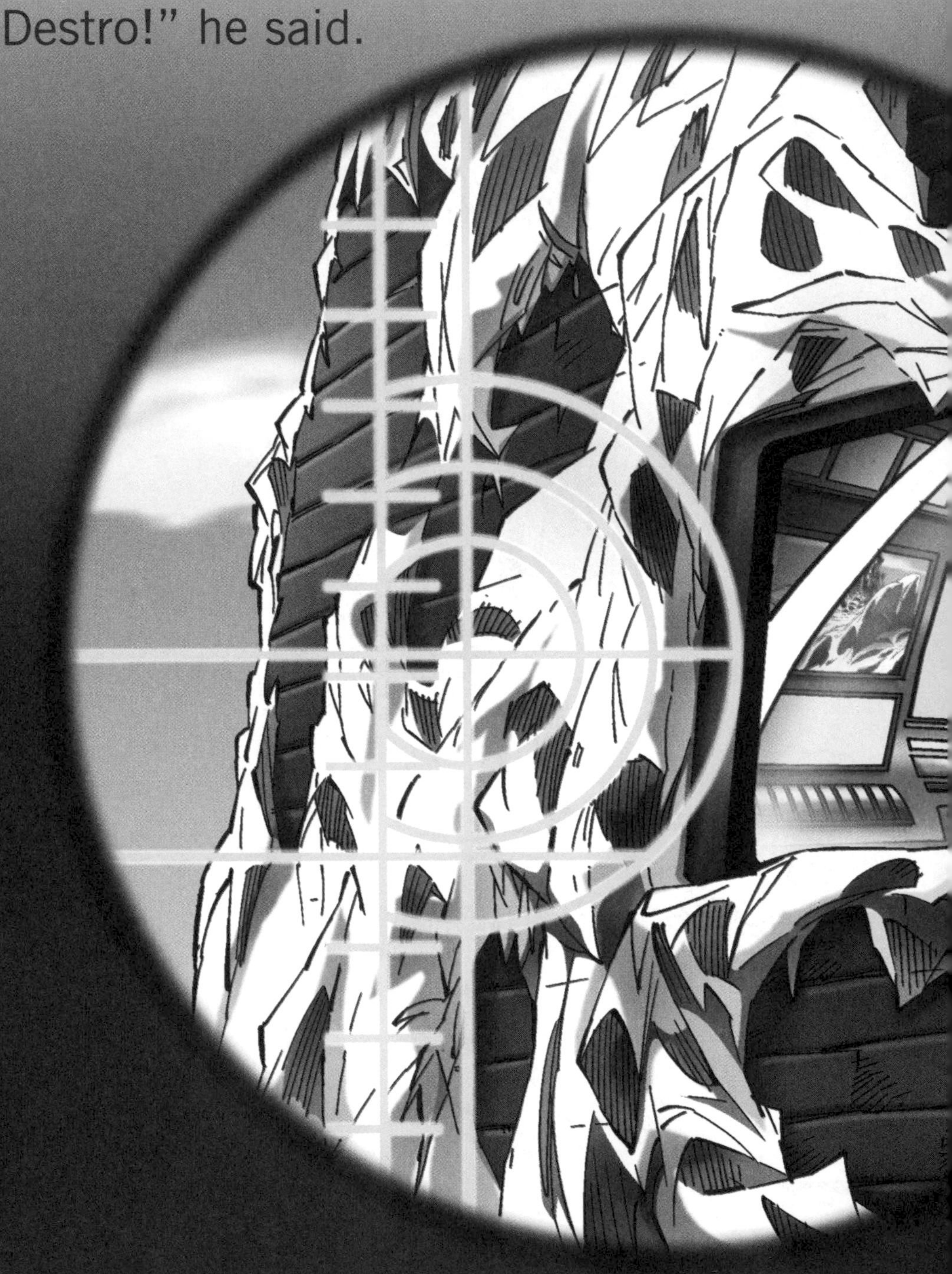

The G.I. JOE team quickly came up with a plan.

Minutes later, Frosbite skied past the tower guards. When the guards chased after him, Duke and Gung-Ho sneaked inside.

"Look at all the gold!" said Duke. "They're melting the ice to mine the precious minerals underneath!"

Then a gang of Neo-Vipers attacked! Duke and Gung-Ho defended themselves with their amazing fighting skills.

COBRA Commander and Destro watched the battle on their monitors.

"The G.I. JOE team found us!" said COBRA Commander. "Our secret plans are ruined — but we'll make them sorry they showed up here!"

The metal doors suddenly slid shut — *CLANG!* — trapping Duke and Gung-Ho inside!

“Attention, intruders!” said COBRA Commander over the loudspeaker. “We have sealed the tower. In ten minutes, the building will blow up. You are doomed!”

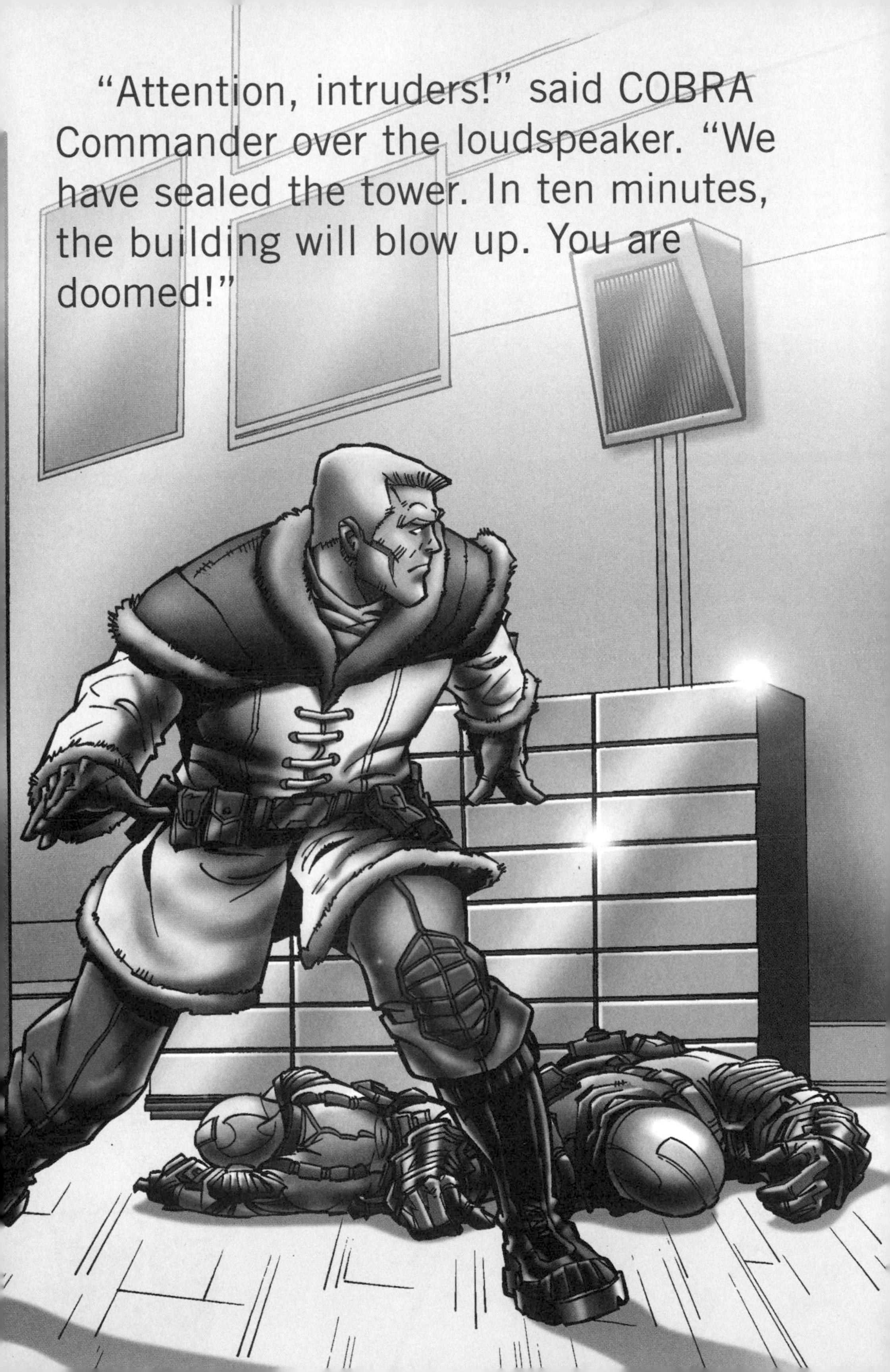

Outside, Frosbite quickly climbed the cliff below the tower. He had to rescue his teammates!

He slipped — but then caught himself before he fell into the canyon far below.

Frostbite reached the tower and smashed through the doors.

Duke and Gung-Ho rushed outside with him.

They ran away from the tower, but had to stop at the edge of a deep canyon.

"There must be a way to escape!" said Duke.

Frostbite had an idea. “We can reverse the laser!” he said. He quickly changed the laser — and fired! Instead of a hot blast, it shot a freeze ray. An ice bridge formed across the canyon.

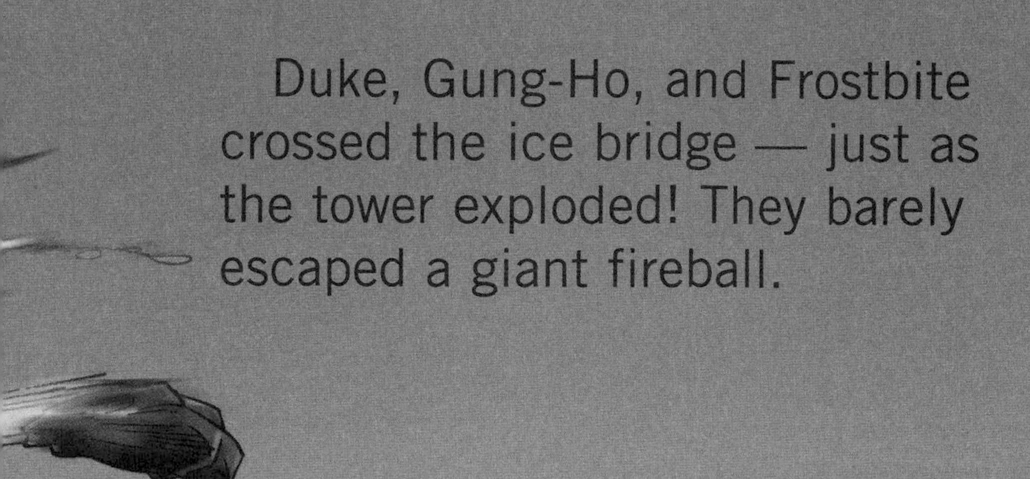

Duke, Gung-Ho, and Frostbite crossed the ice bridge — just as the tower exploded! They barely escaped a giant fireball.

Back at their base, the men looked out at the beautiful land they had saved.

"It was a long day," said Frostbite. "But any day we defeat COBRA is a good day!"

"Yo JOE!"